To my rockababies, Tallulah and Oliver,
and my wife, Kamah, who rocks my world—J.P.

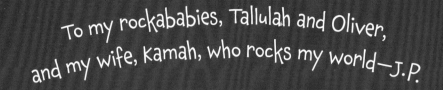

To my parents for ensuring our home was
always rocking at a volume of 11—C.A.

Rock Stars Don't Nap • Text copyright © 2023 by Jason Perkins • Illustrations copyright © 2023 by Cale Atkinson
All rights reserved. Manufactured in Italy. No part of this book may be used or reproduced in any manner whatsoever
without written permission except in the case of brief quotations embodied in critical articles and reviews. For information
address HarperCollins Children's Books, a division of HarperCollins Publishers, 195 Broadway, New York, NY 10007.
www.harpercollinschildrens.com

Library of Congress Control Number: 2023934449
ISBN 978-0-06-315842-9

The artist used Photoshop and a nonstop playlist of rock and roll to create the digital illustrations for this book.
Typography by Erica De Chavez Wong   23 24 25 26 27   RTLO   10 9 8 7 6 5 4 3 2 1   First Edition

Rock Stars DON'T Nap

composed by
Jason Perkins

album art by
Cale Atkinson

HARPER
An Imprint of HarperCollinsPublishers

IN A SMALL HOSPITAL,

in a small town, a BIG STAR was born.

While other babies whimpered and whined, Jimmy's righteous wail shook the nursery all night long.

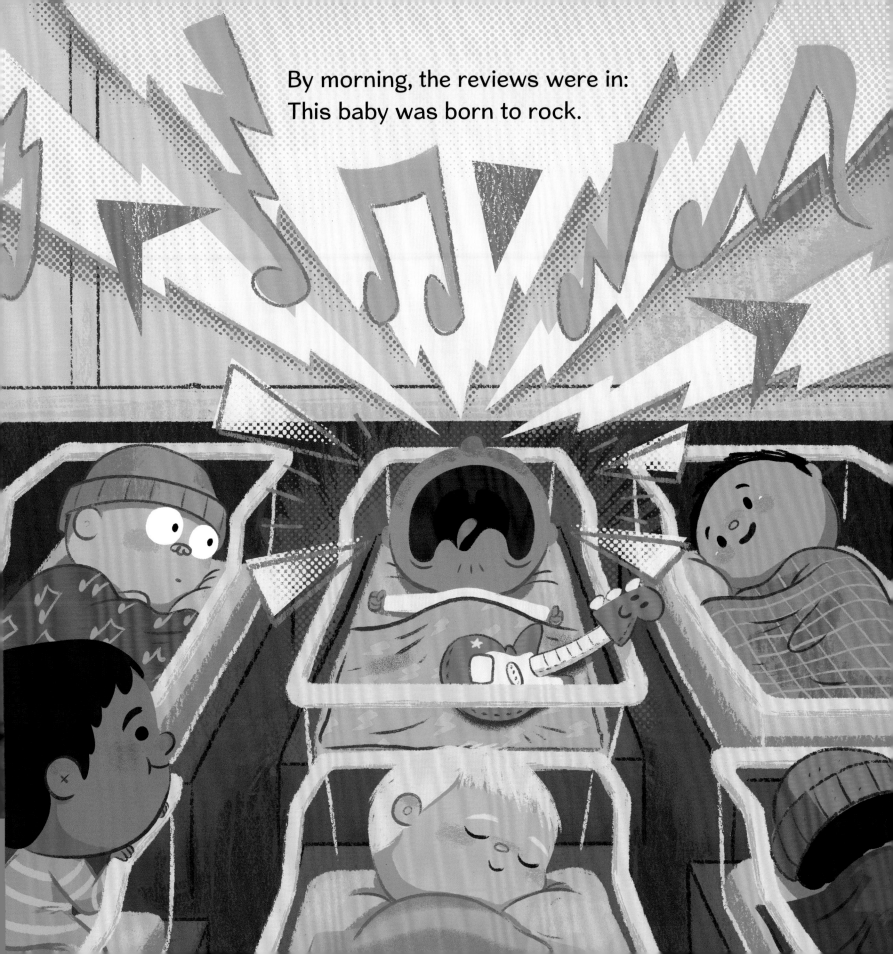

By morning, the reviews were in:
This baby was born to rock.

It wasn't long before Jimmy had Mama rocking around the clock.

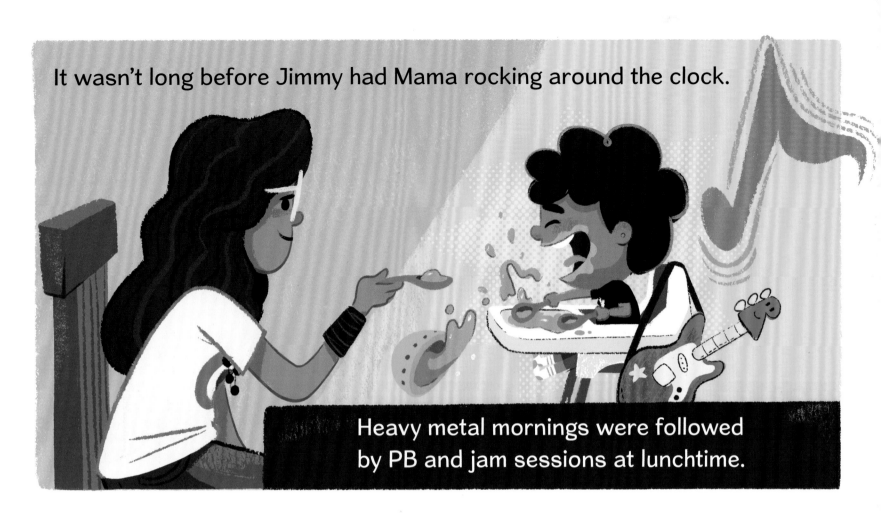

Heavy metal mornings were followed by PB and jam sessions at lunchtime.

Afternoons featured that old-time rock and roll, with a bit of grunge mixed in.

And in the midnight hour, Jimmy's rock operas always brought Mama to her feet.

She was his biggest fan, and together they rocked the nights away.

Soon it was time to take the show on the road.

There were solos at the mall, encores in the park, and back seat ballads all over town.

GO-GO crazy for SALES

By the time Jimmy rolled up to the club, the line was out the door.

Fans crowded around, eager
to meet the pint-sized superstar.
Jimmy shook hands and blew
kisses while they oohed and aahed.

Then he dropped a massive number two hit that left everyone gasping with excitement.

Yes, fame was sweet, but life on the road left Jimmy running on empty.

After a dip in the hot tub and a quick wardrobe change, he was ready to kick back with his biggest fan.

But Mama was singing
a different tune.

Rock stars don't nap!

Jimmy told Mama just that.

This was no way for a rock star to behave.

Mama told Jimmy just that.

It seemed their rocking days were over.

Life as a washed-up rock star wasn't easy. Jimmy began spinning out of control, and he landed on the wrong side of the law.

He mocked the authorities,
threw drinks on the floor, and
scribbled graffiti on the walls.

He even bit the paparazzi!

By showtime,
Jimmy had hit
rock bottom.

Rising up, he vowed to give a performance no one could ignore. He opened with a few classic hits:

But he couldn't draw a crowd.
Jimmy needed something bigger,
something bolder, something LOUDER.
He needed . . .

Mama wasn't feeling it,
and Jimmy was fading fast.

He shredded one last power chord, then capped off his performance with a spectacular stage dive...

Right into the arms
of his biggest fan.

ZZZZZZZZZZZZZZZZZZZZZZZZZZZZZZZZZZ

And together,

ZZZZZZZZZZZZZZZZZZZZZZZZZZZZ

they rocked the night away.

Thanks for rocking with us!

Many of the moments in this story were inspired by classic rock songs. Ask a grown-up to share their favorite hits with you.

Jimmy's Jams

AC/DC. "You Shook Me All Night Long." *Back in Black*, Atlantic, 1980.

Bill Haley & His Comets. "(We're Gonna) Rock Around the Clock." *Rock Around the Clock*, Decca, 1954.

Bob Seger & the Silver Bullet Band. "Old Time Rock and Roll." *Stranger in Town*, Capitol, 1978.

Jackson Browne. "Running on Empty." *Running on Empty*, Asylum Records, 1977.

Europe. "Rock the Night." *The Final Countdown*, Epic, 1985.

The Go-Go's. "Fading Fast." *Beauty and the Beat*, I.R.S. Records, 1981

The Jimi Hendrix Experience. "Come On." *Electric Ladyland*, Reprise, 1968.

Billy Idol. "Rebel Yell." *Rebel Yell*, Chrysalis, 1983.

Chris Isaak. "Baby Did a Bad Bad Thing." *Forever Blue*, Reprise, 1995.

Janis Joplin. "Cry Baby." *Pearl*, Columbia, 1971.

Kiss. "Rock and Roll All Nite." *Dressed to Kill*, Casablanca, 1975.

John Mellencamp. "Small Town." *Scarecrow*, Riva, 1985.

Queen. "Bohemian Rhapsody." *A Night at the Opera*, EMI Electra, 1975.

The Rolling Stones. "Anybody Seen My Baby?" *Bridges to Babylon*, Virgin, 1997.

Jill Sobule. "Rock Me to Sleep." *Pink Pearl*, Beyond, 2000.

Bruce Springsteen. "Born in the U.S.A." *Born in the U.S.A.*, Columbia, 1984.

Survivor. "Eye of the Tiger." *Eye of the Tiger*, Scotti Bros., 1982.